All children have
a great ambition to read
to themselves...

and a sense of achievement when they can do so.
The **read it yourself** *series has been devised to*
satisfy their ambition. Since many children learn
from the Ladybird Key Words Reading Scheme,
these stories have been based to a large extent
on the Key Words List, and the tales chosen are
those with which children are likely to be familiar.

The series can of course be used as supplementary
reading for any reading scheme.

Town Mouse and Country Mouse *is intended for*
children reading up to Book 2c of the Ladybird
Reading Scheme. The following words are
additional to the vocabulary used at that level –

Country, Mouse, lives, Town, house,
stay, quiet, owl, catch, run, away,
supper, do, not, food, bed, my, too,
cannot, sleep, buy, horses, runs, sees,
car, goes, cars, live, park, carpet,
cleaner, hole, cat, Christmas, present

A list of other titles at the same level will be
found on the back cover.

First edition

© LADYBIRD BOOKS LTD MCMLXXXV

Town Mouse and Country Mouse

retold by Alison Ainsworth
illustrated by John Dyke

Ladybird Books Loughborough

This is Country Mouse.

Country Mouse lives
in the country.

He has a home in a
tree.

Here is Town Mouse.

Town Mouse lives in the town.

He has a home in a
town house.

Town Mouse has come
to stay in the country.

Country Mouse says,
I like the country. It is
quiet.

Stay here, Town Mouse, and we can have fun.

This owl wants to
catch Town Mouse.

Town Mouse and
Country Mouse run
away.

Country Mouse says,
Look! Town Mouse,
come into the tree.

Country Mouse and
Town Mouse have
supper.

Town Mouse says, I do not like the food in the country. It is not like the food in the town.

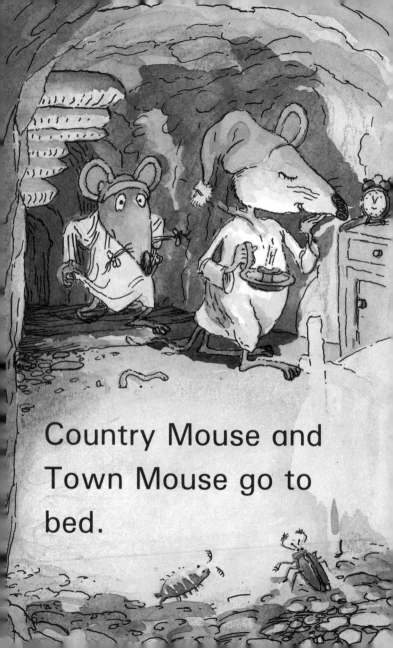

Country Mouse and
Town Mouse go to
bed.

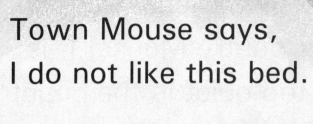

Town Mouse says,
I do not like this bed.

It is not like my bed
in the town.

Town Mouse says to
Country Mouse, It is
too quiet in the country.

I cannot sleep.

Country Mouse has
to look for food.

He says to Town
Mouse, Come and
look for food!

Town Mouse says, No!
In the town we have
shops. We can
buy food.

Some horses come to
see Town Mouse and
Country Mouse.

Town Mouse runs away. He jumps into the water.

Town Mouse says, I do not like the country.

In the town it is not like this.

We do not have horses
in the town. We have
shops in the town.

Come and stay in the
town, Country Mouse,
says Town Mouse.

You can have supper
and go to the shops in
the town.

Town Mouse sees a car.

Look, Country Mouse, he says, we can go to the town in this car.

They jump into the car.

The car goes to the town.

Country Mouse sees the shops.

He sees the cars.

It is not quiet in the town!

Town Mouse says,
I like the town.

My home is not in a
tree.

I live in a town house.

Stay here, Country
Mouse, and we can
have fun.

Town Mouse and Country Mouse have supper.

Country Mouse says,
I do not like the food
in the town.

It is not like the food
in the country.

Town Mouse and
Country Mouse go to
bed.

Country Mouse says,
I do not like this bed.
It is not like my bed
in the country.

Country Mouse says
to Town Mouse, It is
not quiet here.

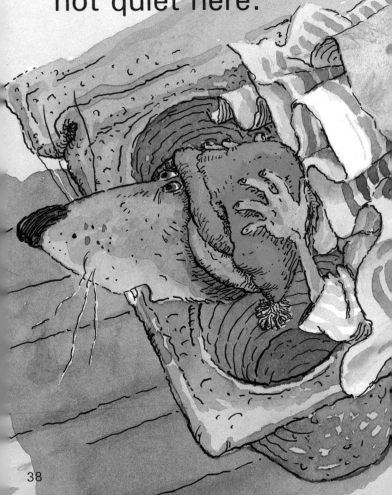

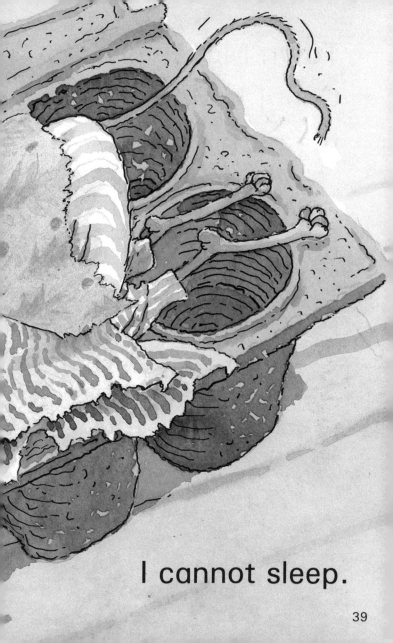

I cannot sleep.

Town Mouse and
Country Mouse go to
the park.

Town Mouse has a
ball. They have fun.

A dog comes for the ball. Country Mouse runs away.

He jumps into the water.

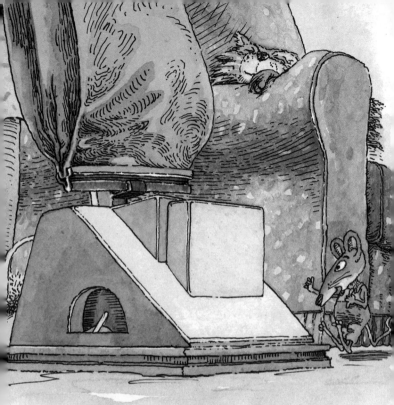

In the town house,
Country Mouse sees
the carpet cleaner.

He runs away.

Town Mouse says,
Here! Country Mouse,
come into the hole.

A cat comes to
catch Town Mouse
and Country Mouse.

They are in the hole.
They have no food.

Country Mouse says,
I want to go home to
the country.

45

Country Mouse sees a
Christmas tree and a
present.

Look! says Town
Mouse, This present is
to go to the country.
You can jump in here
and go home.

The present is in the car. Country Mouse is in the present.

The car goes to the
country.

Country Mouse says,
Here is my home in
the tree.

He says, I do not like
the town.

I am a Country Mouse
and this is my home.